MOJANG

MINECRAFT
WOODSWORD CHRONICLES

DEEP DIVE!

Published in the United States by Random House Children's Books, a division of Penguin Random House LLC, 1745 Broadway, New York, NY 10019, and in Canada by Penguin Random House Canada Limited, Toronto. Random House and the colophon are registered trademarks of Penguin Random House LLC.

rhcbooks.com
minecraft.net

Library of Congress Cataloging-in-Publication Data
Names: Eliopulos, Nick, author. | Flowers, Luke, illustrator.
Title: Deep Dive! / by Nick Eliopulos ; illustrated by Luke Flowers.
Description: New York : Random House, [2019] | Series: Woodsword Chronicles ; book 3
Identifiers: LCCN 2019020376 | ISBN 978-1-9848-5051-5 (hardback) | ISBN 978-1-9848-5052-2 (lib. bdg.) | ISBN 978-1-9848-5053-9 (ebook)
Subjects: | BISAC: JUVENILE FICTION / Media Tie-In. | JUVENILE FICTION / Action & Adventure / General.
Classification: LCC PZ7.E417 Dee 2019 | DDC [Fic]—dc23

Cover design by Diane Choi

Printed in the United States of America
20 19 18 17 16 15 14 13 12

⚙ MOJANG

MINECRAFT
WOODSWORD CHRONICLES

DEEP DIVE!

By Nick Eliopulos
Illustrated by Luke Flowers

Random House 🏠 New York

MORGAN

ASH

HARPER

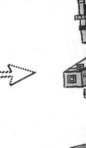

PO

JODI

MS. MINERVA

DOC CULPEPPER

Prologue

IN WHICH X MARKS THE SPOT OF A PLACE NO ONE IN THEIR RIGHT MIND WOULD WANT TO VISIT

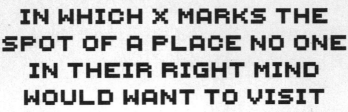

Five figures floated in a vast sea of blue.

Below them was a strange structure. It was unlike anything that existed on earth. Part pyramid and part fortress, it squatted on the seafloor and stretched far into the distance. The structure was a gross shade of green. **It looked almost poisonous.**

But the structure was also grand. It all but dared them to enter.

The figures hovered quietly before it. **They couldn't talk underwater.** But even if they could, the massive monument might have awed

them into silence. The only sounds came from the air bubbles quietly purring, popping, and gurgling around them.

One of them held up a map.

The map showed a big red X.

They all looked from the monument to the map and back again.

The figure with the map put it away and nodded in the direction of the structure. Colorful sea creatures drifted past. The five kicked their legs and swam deeper.

The monument and all its many mysteries awaited.

Chapter 1

SEA TURTLES!
SEA TURTLES, RUN!

Harper Houston held her breath. She strained her eyes in the moonlight. **She knew the white-and-green-speckled eggs sitting in the sand would hatch soon.** And she didn't want to miss a moment of it.

Harper had seen many amazing things over the last several weeks. That's how long she and her friends had been using **special VR headsets** to visit a virtual world. They weren't playing Minecraft anymore. **They were living Minecraft.**

It was all so real. She could feel the sand beneath her feet. She could hear the *snap* and *crackle* of her torch. And she could see cracks appearing on the sea turtle eggs they'd found on the beach.

"I wish I could take a picture of this," her friend Po Chen said. "Can you say 'seashore eggshell selfie' five times fast?" **Po liked to change his appearance in the game.** Tonight he was dressed for the beach, with swim trunks, snorkeling

gear, an inflatable float wrapped around his waist, and a shirt that only a dad would wear.

"I wish I could bring a turtle home with us," said Jodi Mercado. **"I JUST KNOW THEY'RE GOING TO BE ADORABLE."** Jodi was the youngest member of the group. She had a soft spot for animals.

"I WISH THEY'D HURRY UP AND HATCH," Ash Kapoor said. "We can't stay on this beach forever." Ash loved exploration. She wanted to see everything there was to see in this digital land. She didn't do a lot of standing around, either here or in

the real world.

"I wish you would be quiet," Jodi's older brother Morgan said, shushing them. **"IT ISN'T SAFE AT NIGHT. ANYTHING COULD BE OUT THERE."** Morgan played more Minecraft than any of them. His knowledge frequently came in handy. And he was very serious about keeping the others safe.

Harper smiled to herself. All of her friends were wishing for something. She didn't have anything to wish for, though. To her, this moment was perfect just as it was.

THE EGGS HATCHED, ONE AFTER ANOTHER. Tiny baby sea turtles emerged to crawl along the sand. The friends all took a step back.

"That way, little guys," Harper said, pointing to the ocean. **"GO SWIM!"**

Harper knew a bit about real-life sea turtles. She knew that hatchlings immediately made their way across the sand and into the ocean. She assumed Minecraft sea turtles would do the same thing.

"I was right," said Jodi. "They are one hundred percent adorable."

"BUT THEY SOUND WEIRD," Po added.

Harper strained her ears. She heard a low growl nearby. "I don't think that sound is coming from the turtles," she warned.

Morgan hopped in alarm. **"ZOMBIES!"** he cried.

There were four zombies in total. They appeared at the tree line where the forest met the beach. They raised their arms, groaned, and stepped onto the sand.

"WILL THEY HURT THE BABIES?" Jodi asked. She knew less than the others did about Minecraft's hazards. She usually just ran toward the cute mobs and away from the ones she called **yucky.**

"No, they won't," said Ash. **"BECAUSE WE'LL STOP THEM."**

Harper nodded. Ash was right to be confident. As a team, they'd been on several adventures together. **They had built a castle, defeated hostile mobs, and even saved a village by helping some monsters.**

And Harper had a new tool she was eager to try. She held up a bow and lined up her shot.

"Nice!" said Po. "Where'd you get a bow?"

"I MADE IT," Harper answered. "With a few sticks, and strings from a spider's web." For Harper, nothing beat the thrill of making something useful.

Although the thrill of defeating hordes of

zombies came very close.

She let an arrow fly. It met its mark, striking a zombie right in the chest. At the same time, the rest of the group ran forward and attacked with their swords.

"I'LL HAVE TO MAKE BOWS FOR THE REST OF YOU," she said. She fired another arrow.

"It's much nicer fighting those things from a safe distance."

"NO KIDDING!" said Po. He dodged as a zombie swiped at him. "Anytime you want to trade spots, just let me know."

Harper chuckled. She knew Po wasn't in any real danger. It would take more than a few zombies to scare her.

But then **a low moan** sounded at her back.

It didn't make sense. Harper was standing on the beach. She had the ocean behind her. How could anything sneak up on her from that direction?

She turned to see a creature rising from the surface of the water. At first, she thought it was another zombie. But there was something different about it. Its skin was a sickly

shade of blue. Limp strands of seaweed hung from its head.

"IT'S A DROWNED!" cried Morgan.

"A what?" said Harper. She took several quick steps to distance herself from the slimy mob.

"A drowned is like an underwater zombie," Ash shouted from across the beach. She swung her sword at one of the regular zombies.

"It's not underwater at the moment," Harper pointed out.

"It's drawn to the baby turtles," Morgan said. **He jumped to avoid a zombie's grasp.** "Harper, you have to stop it!"

Harper saw that Morgan was right. The drowned was ignoring her and shuffling toward the turtles. **It would catch them before they could make it to the water.**

All of her friends had their hands full. It was up to Harper.

She fired an arrow at the monster's back. **Direct hit!**

The drowned flashed red. It uttered a fearsome groan and turned to face her.

"Well, I got its attention," Harper said. It lurched toward her. **"UH-OH."**

Harper lifted her bow as the creature came at her. But she was out of arrows.

"Don't panic," she said. "You've still got a—"

Harper held up . . . **a loaf of bread.**

Cooked salmon.
A block of wool.

Her square eyes toggled back and forth in exasperation. *I really need to organize my inventory,* she thought.

The drowned was almost close enough to slash her. Leading it away from the baby turtles, she backed up all the way to the line of trees at the edge of the beach.

A low hissing sound came from the forest. **It was the sound of a creeper, about to explode.**

"Oh no," Harper said. She had nowhere to run. The drowned was right in front of her, blocking her escape. She could see past it, though. She watched the baby sea turtles make it to the water. They scuttled into the ocean.

At least she'd been able to save them.

That was her last thought before the creeper blew up.

Chapter 2

GO AHEAD: ROCK THE BOAT!
IT'S ALREADY SUPER
BROKEN.

Po saw it all happen as he raced across the beach. He saw the creeper step out from the trees. He watched as it exploded, knocking Harper all the way to the edge of the water.

He wasn't fast enough to help her. **He just couldn't reach her in time.**

"Harper!" he cried. "Harper, are you all right?"

"Ouch," Harper said. "I actually felt that." She looked down at her blocky hands. "How does that even work? Are the VR goggles interfacing with our nerves? **OR DO THEY JUST TRICK OUR BRAINS INTO THINKING WE FEEL SOMETHING?"**

Po breathed a sigh of relief. "Yeah, you're all right," he said with a smile. "If you're geeking out about the science of being blown up, you're obviously fine."

Po still suspected those VR headsets were more magic than science. He knew better than to say that to Harper, however. She was the brains of the group, particularly when it came to science. She was also a whiz at the crafting table, where she made swords, tools, and more, all from memory.

Morgan, Ash, and Jodi ran up to join them.

"DID YOU SEE HOW THAT CREEPER TOOK OUT THE DROWNED WHEN IT EXPLODED?" Morgan cheered. "That was amazing!"

"I think you mean *scary*," Jodi said. "Harper, you went flying!"

"You should eat some food, Harper," Ash said. "To restore your health."

"At least she's in better shape than the forest," Po said. Where the creeper had exploded, there was a crater in the ground and a big gap in the line of trees. **Blocks of wood, sand, and soil**

floated there for the taking, along with rotten flesh from the drowned.

"We should grab some of this stuff," he said. "Maybe we'll find a use for—"

Po froze. He saw something in the distance. **It was a massive wooden structure.** He could just barely make out the details in the

moonlight. But what he saw **thrilled him.** "Do you guys see that?" he asked.

"What is it?" Jodi asked.

"Something awesome," Po answered. "Team, we just discovered a shipwreck!"

They approached the old shipwreck cautiously. The moon was getting lower in the sky, but night wasn't over yet. **Any number of hostile mobs might be lurking nearby.**

The ship was big. It looked as though it had run aground, crashing into the beach. It showed signs of damage, but it was still in one piece. Its masts rose high into the sky.

"CAN WE BOARD IT?" Po asked. "I want to see what's in there."

Morgan and Ash shared a look. While they all loved Minecraft, Morgan and Ash knew the most about the game.

"What do you think?" Morgan asked her. "I've never found a shipwreck before."

"Me neither," said Ash. **"BUT THEY'RE SUPPOSED TO HOLD TREASURE CHESTS."**

"Well, now we *have* to check it out," Jodi said.

Harper quickly constructed a staircase out of dirt and stone. It would allow them to hop from the beach to the deck of the ship. "We could hack our way in," Harper said. **"BUT THE SHIP LOOKS SO COOL, I DON'T WANT TO BREAK IT."** She peered through a hole in the hull. "Any more than it's already broken, I mean."

They all gathered on the deck. Po immediately pointed out the treasure chest at the front of the ship. He knew from reading nonfiction that **the front of a ship was called the bow.** It was spelled like *bow and arrow* but rhymed with *now* and *wow.*

"There's another chest at the stern," Jodi said, pointing to the back of the ship.

They split up to open the chests. There was a lot of useful stuff inside both chests: carrots

and potatoes, gunpowder and gemstones, and even a couple of pieces of enchanted leather armor.

"NOT BAD FOR A NIGHT'S WORK," Po said.

"And we're not done yet," Morgan said. "Check it out."

Morgan led them down a short staircase to the interior of the ship. There was one more treasure chest waiting to be opened.

"PO, WHY DON'T YOU DO THE HONORS?" Ash suggested. "Since you found the boat."

Po rubbed his blocky hands together. It was like Christmas morning.

He approached the chest, opened it, and looked inside. He saw a faded map, all orange and yellow with a big red **X.** There were also several bottles filled with a dark blue liquid.

"IT'S A TREASURE MAP!" he said, excited. "And some potions."

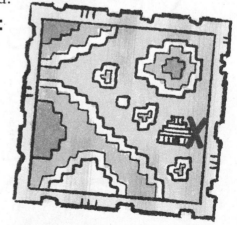

"Those are potions of water breathing," Morgan said. "And the map leads across the ocean."

"Good," Harper said. "If we decide to follow the map, those potions might come in handy."

"WE ARE SO FOLLOWING THE MAP," Po said. "Right?"

"Morgan?" Ash said. "You seem unsure about this."

Morgan brought his square hand up to his chin. He pondered silently for a moment. Finally, he said, "The contents of a chest are supposed to be somewhat random. And this feels . . . not very random." **He paced around in the cramped quarters.**

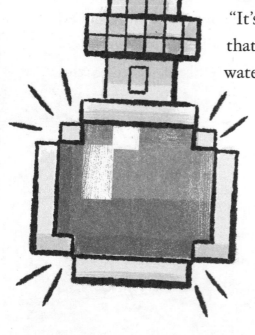

"It's way too convenient that we would find these water-breathing potions right here at the edge of the sea."

Ash nodded slowly in agreement. "I see what you mean. **IT'S CERTAINLY SUSPICIOUS.** On the other hand, maybe we just got lucky."

"We are due some luck," Harper said. "After all, I got blown up a few minutes ago."

"And the fact that we are here, actually in the game, means that **THIS MINECRAFT IS A LITTLE DIFFERENT FROM THE MINECRAFT WE THOUGHT WE KNEW,**" Po added. "We've already seen some mobs acting strangely. Maybe treasure chests are less random in this version of the game."

"Maybe," Morgan said, still thinking.

"DO YOU THINK IT'S A TRICK?" Jodi asked. "A trap?"

Po thought about that. There was a lot they still didn't know about this place. The five of them accessed this virtual world with special VR headsets their science teacher had created. There had been six headsets, **but the sixth headset had gone missing.**

And there had been clues that someone else was in here with them. Someone had stolen materials from them and then used those materials to spell out a warning in big blocky letters: **BEWARE THE**

EVOKER KING!

And someone (or some*thing*) had recently caused a huge migration of zombies and skeletons. The kids had crossed several biomes over the last few visits in their search for answers. They had run out of land now. All they'd found was the ocean.

It felt like a dead end. But the ocean could be crossed. Po wanted to know what was on the other side.

As if reading his mind, Harper quickly expressed that she did *not* feel the same way. **"MAYBE WE SHOULD JUST GO BACK,"** she suggested. "I liked that village. We could raise some more sheep. I could get more practice with the enchanting table."

"Or we could go all the way back to our castle," Jodi added. "We could make it even bigger! And I could create more sculptures."

"That's not really what Minecraft is all about, though—at least for me," Ash said. "Sure, building is fun . . . **BUT I DON'T WANT TO STAY IN ONE PLACE. I ALWAYS WANT TO SEE WHAT'S OUT THERE, BEYOND THE HORIZON."**

"Yes!" Po said. "Especially if there's a treasure map pointing the way. Who knows what we might find?"

"IT COULD BE A TRAP, THOUGH," Morgan said.

Po shrugged. "Then we'll deal with it together."

"AS FRIENDS," Ash said.

Jodi smiled. "That works for me."

"I'm convinced, too," said Harper. "But we should make sure it's unanimous." She turned to Morgan. "What do you say?"

Morgan gazed out over the still-dark horizon, and Po looked over his shoulder. As far as the eye could see, there was only water.

"I say X marks the spot," Morgan said at last.

Chapter 3

DO YOU DARE ENTER THE CELLAR OF SECRETS? NOT WITHOUT A HALL PASS, YOU DON'T!

Jodi was certainly curious about the mysteries of Minecraft. But she had a mystery to solve in the real world, too.

She got to school early the next morning. **She wore her best spy gear: dark sunglasses, quiet sneakers, and a wide-brimmed hat.**

Despite the clothes, Harper still recognized her immediately. "Hey, Jodi," she said. She was sitting on the school's front steps, reading a graphic novel with a dragon on the cover. "Where's Morgan? Don't you usually walk together?"

"He was taking too long to eat breakfast," Jodi

answered. "I had to leave him. I didn't want to, but it was for the greater good!"

Harper grinned. **"On a mission, are you?"**

Jodi looked around the schoolyard, making sure no one was listening. She lowered her voice just to be safe. **"Doc has been acting strange all week.** I'm going to get to the bottom of it."

Doc Culpepper was their science teacher. She was also the inventor of the VR goggles they used to **enter the game world.** (Though she seemed to have no idea what that particular invention was really capable of doing.) For Doc, "acting strange" was actually quite normal.

Jodi and Harper were both fascinated by their teacher. But they were fascinated in different ways. **Harper thought of Doc as a creative and inventive role model who was dedicated to science.** Jodi thought of Doc as a puzzle to be solved—mysterious, secretive, and quite possibly descended from an ancient race of mer-people dedicated to taking over the surface world.

"Does your investigation have room for an apprentice?" Harper asked. "Maybe I could help out."

Jodi gave Harper a grateful smile. She also gave Harper her hat. "Glad to have you on board," Jodi said, "because that hat is way too big for me!"

Jodi led Harper to a staircase. **The stairs descended into a dark basement.**

"Why are we going down here?" Harper asked. "Doc's lab is on the ground floor."

"That's what made me suspicious," Jodi said. "I've seen Doc go down here three times this week. Each time, she was carrying buckets full of water."

"That *is* strange," Harper said. She held the handrail, careful not to lose her footing in the low light. "Do you think it's for a science experiment?"

"No," said Jodi. **"I think she's building a basement swimming pool. Or an ice-skating rink!"** She frowned. "Although I have to admit, your idea does sound more likely."

They reached the bottom of the stairs. There was a large furnace on one side of the room. Against the back wall was a large closet with a chain-link door. In the closet, cleaning supplies were neatly stacked upon the floor-to-ceiling metal shelves.

"Do you smell that?" Harper asked.

Jodi sniffed the air. "It smells like . . . the beach?"

"It's salt water," Harper said.

"Of course!" Jodi said. "Harper, **what if Doc is from Atlantis?** That would explain why her science is so advanced!"

Harper gave Jodi a funny look. "She went to college and got two doctorate degrees," said Harper. **"That explains why her science is so advanced."**

"Maybe she went to college . . . in Atlantis?" Jodi suggested.

"Maybe," Harper said. She pointed at a series of small puddles leading down a side hallway. "The trail leads that way."

They walked to the end of the short hallway. A door was ajar. **Jodi peered inside.**

"What do you see?" Harper whispered.

"It looks like a classroom," Jodi whispered. "But there are big tanks of water. **And I think I hear something.** An animal, scuttling and *squeaking.*"

Jodi strained her ears. Just then, a shrill noise sounded out. It was so loud and unexpected that Jodi nearly screamed.

"We must have tripped an alarm!" she hissed over the noise. **"Sharkmen are probably already on their way to detain us! We** have to get out of here!"

"No, wait," Harper said. She reached into her backpack and pulled out . . . a phone.

A moment later, the door swung open. Doc stood in the doorframe. "What in the name of Ada Lovelace's morning tea is going on out here?" she asked.

"Sorry!" Harper said. She seemed to be apologizing to both Jodi and Doc at the same time. **"I just got my sister's hand-me-down smartphone.** I guess I forgot to turn the sound off."

Jodi slapped her own forehead. Harper was talented at many things, but apparently she was not much of a spy.

"But what are you two doing down here at all?" Doc asked. "I didn't miss the morning bell again, did I?"

"We, uh, we were . . ." Jodi fumbled for an excuse.

"We were just curious," Harper said. She gave Jodi a look that said *We may as well be honest, right?*

Jodi shrugged. "Yeah. I saw you yesterday with a bucket of water."

"Ah, yes," Doc said. **"Well, the mermaids**

do get very thirsty. . . ."

Jodi vibrated with excitement. "You've got *mermaids* down here?"

Doc chuckled. "I'm just teasing. **No, I have something better than mermaids.** Come and take a look."

The girls followed Doc into a room that smelled strongly of the sea. It looked very much like her classroom lab, but it was bigger. There were a dozen long black tables, and each table held a large aquarium. The aquariums were filled with water but otherwise empty. And in the back of the room . . .

"**Baron Sweetcheeks!**" Jodi cried, spotting the class hamster in his cage. "What is he doing here?"

SWEETCHEEKS

"Minerva let me borrow him," Doc answered. "It gets lonely down here. **And science needs observers.**"

The hamster lapped water from his water bottle. Jodi thought he looked extra adorable today. Then she noticed the aquarium beside him. Unlike the others, it was full of life. **Small fish darted back and forth** above a colorful seabed.

"What kind of science are you doing?" asked Harper. **"It looks like you've re-created a little slice of the ocean."**

"That's right," said Doc. **"This is just the start of a great experiment.** Tomorrow, I'll remove pieces of coral from the main aquarium. The coral will be transferred to the other tanks you see all around you."

"That's coral?" Jodi asked. She took a closer

look. She'd thought the seabed was mostly rocks. Up close, however, the material looked somewhat bony or shell-like. It grew in interesting shapes—swirls and branches. The mix of colors was strikingly beautiful.

"It's like a whole reef!" Jodi continued. **She'd seen pictures in books of great coral reefs, environments where ocean life thrived.** The images always reminded her of the rain forest, but underwater.

"This is for an experiment?" Harper said. Her eyes drank in all the color. **"Can we help?"**

Doc smiled. "I was hoping you'd offer. In fact, for a project this big, I'll need the help of your entire class."

Jodi said, **"Cool!"**

Harper said, "Great!"

Suddenly, Harper's backpack made a shrill electronic chirping sound again.

"Oops! Sorry!" she said, and **she slapped her backpack until the phone went silent.**

Chapter 4

SMOOTH SAILING!
(THE "MOO" PART WILL
MAKE SENSE EVENTUALLY.)

As morning dawned in Minecraft, Harper and her friends built their first boats.

It was Ash's great idea to use old wood planks from the shipwreck. That way, they wouldn't have to use up any of the wood from their inventories. It also felt poetic to make small boats out of the large one. The ship was landlocked, but pieces of it would be sailing the ocean once more.

The crafting formula was quite simple. In a matter of moments, **five small rowboats bobbed in the water.**

"I wish we could all share a boat," Morgan said.

"Boats here can only hold a single person," Ash said. "But we'll travel together. Everyone will stay close."

"ARR, DAYLIGHT'S WASTING," Po said. He was dressed as a pirate, complete with captain's hat and a black beard. He hopped into his birchwood boat. "Shove off!"

"Shove off?" echoed Jodi.

"IT'S SAILOR TALK," Harper said. "It means 'Let's go, already.'"

"Oh." Jodi giggled and climbed into her own boat. "In that case: Aye, aye!"

ASH WAS NERVOUS AT FIRST. She had been on boats in real life, and the rocking motion had made her seasick. That wasn't a problem here, though. **The sea was calm and quiet,** like a great glistening blue carpet.

They talked about school, and Po's basketball team, and how excited Harper was for Doc's coral assignment. Before they knew it, the sun was setting.

"There's nowhere to put down a bed out here," Morgan said.

"BUT THERE AREN'T ANY MOBS TO WORRY ABOUT, EITHER," Ash pointed out. "We may as well keep going."

So they traveled through the night, gliding onward by the light of the moon.

When daylight had come again, Morgan checked the map. **"WE STILL HAVE A LONG WAY TO GO,"** he said.

Ash felt a desire to be useful. "We may as well

do some fishing," she suggested. "Who has the fishing rod?"

"That'd be me, matey," said Po. He steered over to her and placed the rod in her boat. **Harper had enchanted it, so it was quite easy to use.** Along with bread and apples, cooked fish had quickly become their main source of food. Raw fish wasn't as filling, but it was better than nothing. And Ash wanted to be sure they had plenty to eat. **She was a Wildling Scout.** That meant she liked to be prepared for anything.

They settled into a comfortable silence, and the sun moved steadily across the sky. The days were short here, and the nights were even shorter.

They kept going.

On the fourth day, Po cried, **"LAND HO!"**

Ash turned her head to look where Po was pointing. He was right—land! "Is that where we're headed, Morgan?" she asked.

Morgan was already consulting their map. "No," he said. "We still have a distance to go. But I can see that **landmass on the map.** It's a small island." He shrugged. "We may as well check it out. I'd like to set up our beds and reset our spawn point."

"We should probably disconnect soon, anyway," Harper added. **"THIS IS THE LONGEST WE'VE BEEN IN THE GAME WITHOUT TAKING A BREAK."**

"Harper's excited to get to her homework," Jodi teased.

"That's not true!" Harper said. "Although tonight's long-division worksheet does look

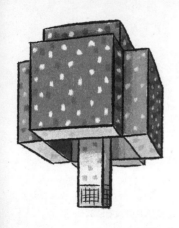

deliciously challenging. . . ."

"ARR!" Po cried. "ANY MORE TALK OF HOMEWORK AND I'LL HAVE YE SWABBIN' THE DECK."

They made landfall just as the sun set. The ground was a strange shade of gray, and **huge mushrooms** towered above them.

"What is this place?" asked Jodi.

"IT'S A MUSHROOM ISLAND!" Po said. Ash noticed he was so excited that he forgot to talk like a pirate. "And that means we might see *the best animal of all time*!"

"A llama?" Jodi guessed hopefully. **She really liked llamas.**

"No," said Po. "Better."

"A panda?" Jodi said. "A dolphin? A monkey? A dog? A dog wearing a silly outfit?" She really liked pandas, dolphins, monkeys, dogs, and dogs wearing silly outfits. **Who didn't?!**

Ash laughed. "You have a lot of favorite animals, Jodi."

"But nothing you've seen in real life can prepare

you for *that*," Po said, pointing.

A mob rounded a corner, stepping into view. **It looked like a cow,** but it was spotted red and white, with tiny mushrooms growing along its back.

"What . . . ," said Jodi. "What *is* that marvelous, wonderful, lovable creature?"

"MOOSHROOM!" Po cried, and he leapt for joy. "Someone give me some wheat! Hurry, hurry!"

Ash cycled through her inventory. **She found a sheaf of wheat and dropped it on the ground.** Po snatched it up and ran toward the speckled, big-eyed animal.

He waved the wheat in front of the mooshroom's face. That got its attention. Now, as **Po ran around the small island,** the mooshroom followed wherever he went.

"Me next!" Jodi cried. "Me next!" She followed the mooshroom, who followed Po, and that made everyone laugh.

Then a dark shadow loomed over them. And then another and another.

Ash looked up. By the light of the moon, she could just make out a trio of flying shapes. "Are those bats?" she asked.

"It's hard to tell," Harper said. **"BUT I THINK THEY'RE TOO BIG TO BE BATS."**

"Oh no," Morgan said. "Jodi! Po! Get over here!"

The smiles dropped immediately from Ash's and Jodi's faces. They recognized the seriousness in Morgan's voice. "What is it, brother?" Jodi asked.

"Find cover!" he said. **"THOSE ARE PHANTOMS. AND THEY'RE COMING OUR WAY!"**

Chapter 5

TERROR IN THE SKIES! DANGER IN THE DEPTHS! WHAT ELSE IS NEW?

Morgan got a good look at the first phantom as it swooped low over the island.

At first, it did look batlike. But it was much larger than a bat from the real world, and **its wings were tattered like an old, ragged curtain.** Morgan could see white bones sticking out through its broken blue skin. Its eyes glowed an eerie shade of green.

The phantom looked dangerous. And it was.

It swooped low, slashing into Jodi. She flared red, a sign that she'd taken damage.

"OW!" she said. **"I FELT THAT!"**

The phantom returned to the sky after hitting her. Along with the other two phantoms, it circled high above their heads.

"There's nowhere to hide!" said Po. "Harper, get your bow out!"

"IT'S USELESS," Harper said. "I don't have any arrows. I can't make more without feathers!"

"We can fight back with swords," said Ash. "We just have to wait for the phantoms to swoop down at us."

"THAT'S TOO RISKY," Morgan said. "Jodi's already hurt. How many more hits can she take?"

"I'm fine," Jodi argued, but **she sounded scared.**

Fighting was dangerous. The island didn't provide any shelter. The boats were too slow for a getaway.

Morgan had only one idea for how they could escape the phantoms. But he wasn't sure it was a very good idea.

Then one of the phantoms broke from the pack. It dove for them.

It was now or never.

"Everyone into the water!" Morgan cried.

He waited just long enough to make sure Jodi made it to the edge of the island. **Then they all jumped, splashing into the water together.**

At first, Morgan couldn't see much. Everything beneath the surface was a hazy blue. But as he went

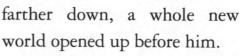

farther down, a whole new world opened up before him.

Colorful schools of Minecraft fish darted through the water. An entire forest of long strands of kelp waved in the currents. In the distance, **a squid** sped through the water using its tentacles.

It was a beautiful sight. But one thing was missing: air to breathe.

Morgan blinked twice, an action that brought up a menu. His health and hunger meters were full, but **his air was already half gone.**

He took out a potion of water breathing. Before he could drink it, Ash swam in front of him and shook her head.

Morgan didn't understand. **The potions were only a temporary solution,** but they were better than nothing.

Ash gestured for Morgan and the others to follow her. She pointed at something in the water. Something moving.

It was a great column of bubbles. **The bubbles rose from a glowing orange square of magma** on the seafloor. They floated all the way to the surface. And inside the column of bubbles . . .

He could breathe! Morgan took a big breath, then looked above and below him. In the light cast by the magma block, he could see the others had all made it safely to the bubbles.

He could also see the shadows of the phantoms. They were still circling above the surface, **like hungry sharks**.

Morgan breathed a sigh of relief that there weren't any *actual* sharks in Minecraft. Of course, there were other underwater dangers—but it was best not to think about that right now.

They needed a shelter. He swam over to

Harper. **She was the fastest builder.** And she usually remembered **the recipes and formulas that Morgan forgot.**

He raised his hands. He tried to make his arms look like a triangular roof over his head. *Shelter*, he thought at her. *Come on, Harper. Let's get building!*

Harper just gave him a blank look. She shook her head and shrugged. She couldn't understand him.

Morgan decided he'd just have to do it himself. **But he had precious few materials in his inventory.** He swam to the seafloor and began digging up dirt, then piling it to make the foundations of a house.

It was taking forever. Each time he placed a few blocks, **he had to return to the bubbles for more air.**

Finally, Ash seemed to realize what he was doing. She shook her head at him and gestured toward a nearby wall of rock. *Of course,* he thought. Building up against **an existing wall would save on materials.**

Ash started placing glass blocks along the

underwater cliff. **She had enough glass to create a single enclosed room.** Actually, it was more like an elevator shaft than a room. It had no ceiling. Instead, it went all the way up to the surface of the water. That was risky, because she had to swim up to where the phantoms could reach her. **But it also allowed her to take gulps of air.** And she was quick, never staying at the surface for more than a moment.

In a little while, she was done. She had built the structure around herself, so she was on the inside when it was finished.

Morgan gestured at her through the glass. *Okay,* he tried to say. *That's shelter. But it's still full of water.* **Ash would run out of air in seconds!**

Instead of kicking to the surface for another breath, Ash pulled out a white material. It was wool. She began filling the interior with blocks of the fluffy white stuff.

Morgan had no idea why she was doing that.

Soon the structure was so full of wool that Ash had no room to move.

Then she held up her flint.

She struck a spark.

And the wool went up in flames.

Ash was in the center of a roaring inferno!

Morgan tried to scream her name. When he opened his mouth, however, no sound came out. Only a rush of bubbles.

Chapter 6

UNEXPECTED LAB PARTNERS (AND OTHER DISASTERS)

Harper was in full-on panic mode even *before* Ash's avatar caught on fire.

Despite the column of bubbles all around her, she felt like she couldn't breathe.

What would happen to Ash if she ran out of health here? Harper hated that she didn't know the answer to that question. **She desperately wanted to understand the science that made this place work.**

She swam toward Ash with a loaf of bread in her hand. It was all she could think of to do.

But Ash waved her away. She was standing on the other side of the glass wall. The fire had burned away—and so had the water. **Ash had created a shelter, a little pocket of air at the bottom of the sea.** And she was still standing. She was okay.

They watched as Ash placed a door in her structure. Once she had finished, Harper was the first one inside.

"Ash, that was brilliant!" she said. "Clearing out all the water by burning wool. How did you think of that? YOU SHOULD EAT SOMETHING!"

Ash munched on bread while the others entered the structure. It was cramped but dry.

"I only wish I had thought of a way to do it *without* getting caught in the fire," Ash said. "But I knew I had enough health to handle it."

"IT WAS SCARY TO SEE IT HAPPEN, THOUGH," said Morgan. "I'm glad you're okay."

"And this place is awesome!" Jodi said. "It's like a reverse aquarium."

"I suppose the view is nice," Ash agreed. "More important, there's room for our beds."

"So we can finally disconnect for the day," Jodi said with relief. She poked Harper playfully.

"AND GET TO THAT HOMEWORK."

"Arr," Po groaned, sounding like the saddest pirate in the world.

The next morning, Harper woke and immediately started thinking about the previous day's adventure. **She couldn't shake the feeling that she'd disappointed her friends** when they'd been underwater.

Morgan had looked to her to figure things out. He'd expected her to have solutions. But she'd just panicked. **And because of that, Ash had put herself in harm's way.**

She decided that would never happen again.

In quiet moments throughout the day, Harper used her phone to go online. She read everything she could about **Minecraft's aquatic environments.** Much of the information was new to her.

"Kelp is really useful," she told Morgan at lunch. "Among other things, we can dry it out and eat it.

It's so abundant, **we'll never go hungry!"**

"That's great," said Morgan.

"And there are dolphins. If we feed them fish, they might lead us to treasure."

"We already have a treasure map, though," Ash said.

"In real-life news, that math homework was *rough*," Po said. "Harper, what did you get for the last problem? Please tell me it was a whole number between 422 and 424."

"Oh." Harper felt her cheeks go warm. **"I didn't do the homework yet."**

"You what?!" Po said. This was totally unexpected news. "Harper, it's due later today!"

"I know, I know," she said.

She put away her phone and pulled out her homework. "I'll do it now. I have plenty of time."

She saw her friends exchange a look.

"Harper, were you reading about Minecraft all night?" Morgan asked. "Instead of doing the assignment?"

"I was actually trying to make this clunky old

phone work better," Harper answered. "But I may have spent some time reading about Minecraft as well." She bit her lip. **"I JUST WANT TO BE PREPARED NEXT TIME. THAT'S ALL."**

Ash opened her mouth to speak, but she was interrupted by **the sound of a tremendous crash.** The kids all looked over to see their

homeroom teacher, Ms. Minerva. The teacher was trying to shove a closet door closed. She leaned against it with her full weight. But the closet was too full.

"Oh, it's hopeless," Ms. Minerva said. She let the door swing open, and **dozens of colorful plastic cafeteria trays clattered out onto the floor.**

"Is everything okay, Ms. Minerva?" Ash asked.

Ms. Minerva blew a frizzy strand of hair out of her face. "Everything's fine," she said. "I just need to find a place to stash all these old trays. The PTA bought the school new ones."

"Why not just throw them away?" asked Po.

"They're not recyclable," Ms. Minerva said. **"SO THEY'D END UP IN A LANDFILL SOMEWHERE.** I'm determined to find a use for them. But first I need to get them out of the way."

"I can help," offered Harper.

"The *rest of us* can help," Ash said. "You should finish your assignment."

Harper almost argued, but she knew Ash was right. She nodded. "Thanks, Ash."

Harper spent the rest of her lunch period finishing her homework. She lost track of time and arrived a few minutes late to science class.

"Ah, Harper!" Doc said as Harper stepped into the basement lab. **"Good. Now we have an even number."**

Harper scanned the room. The whole class had paired off. Morgan was with Ash. Jodi was with Po.

"You'll be Theo's lab partner," said Doc.

Harper nodded mutely. She was disappointed not to be with one of her friends. But it was her own fault for being late. She didn't know Theo well, but she gave him a polite smile as she sat at his table.

"Today is the big day," said Doc. **"Welcome to Project Coral Restoration."**

Harper felt a little thrill at that.

Doc circulated among the class. **She gave each student a petri dish** containing a long piece of coral.

"All around the world, coral populations are in grave danger," Doc explained. "Due to global warming, oceans are getting warmer. And that causes big problems for sea life. Especially for coral, which is very fragile. **Entire reefs are dying.**"

Harper chewed on her pencil. She often worried about the impact humans had on the environment. Every time she learned about another endangered species, her heart hurt.

"But there's good news," Doc continued.

"Experiments have shown that coral reefs can be restored. This is done in a variety of ways. The most common way is to grow new coral in laboratories like this one. When the coral is strong enough, it's transported to the ocean."

Harper gazed down at her petri dish. Her piece of coral shimmered with droplets of salt water.

"I'd like us to perform an experiment," said Doc. "Each of you has an identical piece of coral. **I'd like you to place your coral in your aquarium and measure its growth.** Everyone's water will be slightly different. Yours might be warmer, saltier, or more acidic than your neighbor's. In this way, we'll determine the best conditions for growing this particular type of coral. **So let's get started!"**

"Awesome," Theo said, grinning at Harper. "This should be fun."

"I don't know about *fun*," Harper said. "It sounds very serious to me."

Theo dropped his smile. "Sure, the problem is serious," he agreed. "But maybe we'll be the ones to help fix it."

Harper liked the sound of that. "You're right," she said. "I'm sorry. **I didn't mean to be negative."**

Harper tried to stay optimistic. She knew science often held the answers to some of the world's biggest and scariest problems. That's why **she loved science** to begin with.

Some days, though, it felt like the problems kept piling up.

Chapter 7

EVERYTHING LOOKS BETTER BY THE LIGHT OF A SEA PICKLE.

"I CAN'T BELIEVE PO IS MISSING THIS,"** said Jodi. "And for basketball practice!"

"He *likes* basketball practice," said Morgan.

"Yeah," said Jodi. "But is anything better than this?"

Jodi pointed past the glass wall of their base under the sea. There was a whole world to explore out there. And she wouldn't miss out on that for anything.

Since Po wasn't with them, **they'd all agreed not to travel too far.** They needed to return to their base at the end of the day. That way, they would all still spawn in the same place when Po rejoined them.

Ash insisted they needed to stock up on supplies, anyway. **Between their recent battles and the long boat ride, they'd gone through a lot of their stuff.**

And Morgan liked the idea of scouting the area. They could check for any problems or dangers nearby. Then they would know what to expect when they started to follow the map again.

"I THINK THE MAP IS LEADING US SOMEWHERE UNDERWATER," said Morgan. "We can probably swim the rest of the way."

"Soon," Ash said. "For today, let's just see what there is to see."

As it turned out, there was a lot to see.

Now that she wasn't fleeing from phantoms, Jodi was able to take in the beauty of her surroundings. **She was surprised at how alive the ocean was.** There was movement everywhere, from darting schools of fish to swaying sea grass.

Her heart leapt for joy when a dolphin approached them. It seemed as curious about them as she was about it. **Jodi noticed that she**

swam a little faster when the dolphin was nearby. She tried to keep up with it, but after a while it darted away.

Po would be sorry he missed that.

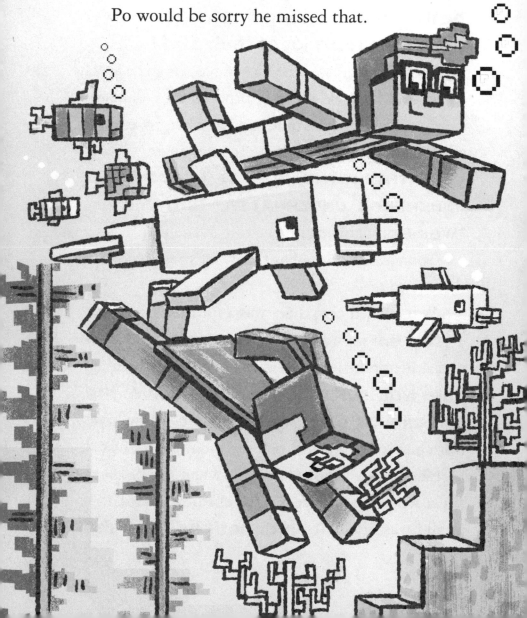

They'd each drunk a potion of water breathing. As a backup, Harper brought along **a block of magma.** If they needed air, she could place the magma on the ground and produce another column of bubbles.

But there was plenty of magma already in the area. It was easy to spot, softly glimmering orange in the distance. And the magma wasn't the only source of underwater light. Every now and then, they found small, **glowing green cylinders.**

Harper had told her about them earlier in the day. **They were called sea pickles, and Jodi thought they were wondrous.**

But by far, Jodi's favorite thing was the coral. These weren't the small, fragile pebbles she'd seen in Doc's class. They looked like great tree branches, and they came in every color of the rainbow. **She took every piece she found.** She was sure she'd find a use for them, even if they were only good for decoration.

After a while, Morgan signaled that they should turn around.

As they swam back, **Jodi made a mental list of everything she needed** to tell Po about. When their undersea base came into view, she was surprised to see a figure standing inside of it. It had to be Po! Maybe he'd gotten out of basketball practice early?

But when they swam up to the base, nobody was there.

"THAT'S REALLY STRANGE," Jodi said once they were safely inside the structure. "I could have sworn I saw somebody through the glass."

Morgan shrugged. **"MAYBE IT WAS A TRICK OF THE LIGHT."**

"No, I think Jodi is right," Ash said as she lifted the lid of the group's treasure chest. "Someone was here."

"What makes you say that?" Harper asked.

"I STASHED A FEW THINGS IN THIS CHEST before we left. I wanted to free up room in my inventory."

Morgan hopped in place. "Did somebody steal from us again?"

Ash shook her head. "The opposite. Somebody put stuff in here. **THERE ARE MORE POTIONS OF WATER BREATHING.** And scute."

Morgan's jaw dropped.

"WHAT IS SCUTE?" Jodi asked.

Ash held up a small green orb. "It's a material dropped by baby turtles when they grow up. It can be used to make a special helmet."

"A helmet that helps you hold your breath while underwater," added Morgan.

"MAYBE THIS IS ALL JUST A GLITCH?" Jodi suggested.

"Or maybe whoever is in here with us wants to help," said Harper.

"But if that's true, why be sneaky about it?" Morgan said. He shook his head. **"SORRY, BUT I STILL THINK WE'RE BEING LED INTO A TRAP."**

"No offense," said Jodi, "but for once, I hope you're wrong."

Morgan gazed out through the glass. "Me too," he said.

Chapter 8

SCIENTIFIC SUCCESS! AWKWARD PERSONAL MOMENTS!

By Monday, Harper and Theo's coral had already started to grow.

"It's incredible!" Harper said. She double-checked their log. "If it keeps growing at this rate, our coral will be ready for ocean transport in a few weeks."

Although they had started with a single piece of coral, Doc had asked them to break the coral into smaller pieces. She had explained that **breaking the coral would cause it to grow faster.**

Some of the pieces had only grown a couple of millimeters. Some had grown by centimeters. But they were all growing.

Theo looked around at his classmates' aquariums. **"Our samples are definitely doing the best."** He grinned shyly. "Not that it's a competition."

"Right," said Harper. Then she grinned back. **"But that *is* pretty cool."**

Harper snuck a peek at a neighboring aquarium. Theo was right. Not everyone was having the same success. She made sure to write down the exact temperature of their water. They also recorded the pH level and the salinity. If their coral continued to do well, **those numbers would be important to scientists all over the world.**

"Hey," Theo said. "Are you playing Minecraft after school today?"

Harper froze. "Uh, why?" she asked.

Theo shrugged. "Isn't that what you and your friends do in **the computer lab after school?** I saw you go in there every day last week. My locker's right there."

"Oh," Harper said. "Yeah. We play Minecraft and stuff."

"I'm a gamer, too," he said. "I've put some of my builds online. You should check them out."

"Yeah," Harper said. "I definitely will. Definitely!"

An awkward silence followed. Harper had a feeling Theo was waiting for an invitation. But she couldn't bring someone new into the group, could she? For one thing, they didn't have an extra headset. For another, there was real danger in that virtual world. She'd felt it when that creeper had exploded. **How could she put someone else in harm's way?**

"Oh!" Harper said. "I totally forgot. I was supposed to refill Baron Sweetcheeks's water today."

It wasn't technically true. But Harper felt more and more awkward the longer the silence lasted. And the class hamster could always use fresh water.

She took her time with the task. She was still at the hamster cage when the bell rang and students started filing out of the classroom.

When she walked back to her table, **Theo was already gone.** She felt guilty. She didn't like keeping secrets from anyone. But the idea of inviting someone new into their special group would have to be discussed by everyone.

As she put her books into her backpack, she noticed something strange. **It looked like a piece of coral was missing from their aquarium.**

That can't be, she thought. But Theo had their logbook, so she couldn't double-check.

She'd have to look into it tomorrow.

Chapter 9

WHERE'S THE REFEREE? BECAUSE THAT FASHION IS TOTALLY OUT OF BOUNDS!

Basketball was taking more and more of Po's time.

Po played on a mixed ability team. That meant every player on his team used a wheelchair during practice and games, even though some of his teammates didn't use wheelchairs otherwise. Woodsword was one of several schools in the state with a mixed ability team, so Po got to travel to

nearby cities for weekend games.

Po liked being on a team. **In fact, he was the star player.** But it didn't leave much time for trying other things. He worried that he would let his teammates down if he took time away from basketball to be in the school play, or run for class president, or—

SWOOSH!

Po sank another basket from the three-point line. His teammates all cheered, and Po forgot his worries for a moment. He was happy to be right where he was.

Practice ended a few minutes

later. **Po checked the time and saw that it was once again too late to join the Minecraft crew.** They would all have disconnected by the time he got to the lab. But if he hurried, he might get to hear about what he'd missed.

Po looked over at his teammate Ricky. **A flash of color caught Po's eye.** Ricky was wearing a necklace.

That wasn't too unusual. While nobody was allowed to wear jewelry during a game, the rules were less strict at practice.

But Po could swear he'd seen the necklace before. Not in a jewelry case . . . but in an aquarium.

"Hey, Ricky," he said. "Where'd you get that necklace?"

Ricky smiled. "You like it?"

"Sure," Po said, starting to get a bad feeling. **"But . . . that's coral, isn't it?"**

"It sure is," Ricky said. "I'm from Puerto Rico, so **it's like a little piece of home.** I bought it from a kid in my math class."

Po frowned. He couldn't be sure, but it looked just like a piece of coral from Doc's experiment.

But why would anyone sell off a piece of their science project?

He wanted to ask for the seller's name. But their conversation had drawn attention. Several of their teammates came over to admire Ricky's jewelry.

"Looks good, Rick," said one of them.

"It'd look better on me!" said another.

"I can hook you guys up," Ricky said. "Maybe we can get a team discount."

Po's stomach soured. **He was pretty sure that plucking coral from seawater and putting it on a string wasn't good for the environment.** He tried to say so.

But he was totally drowned out by the team's excitement.

Chapter 10

UNDER WATER.
UNDER PRESSURE.
UNDER ATTACK!

With Po's return the next day to the world of Minecraft, the group had everything they needed to reach the map's destination.

"Finally," Jodi said. "My patience meter has been depleted for days!"

"I wonder what we'll find," said Harper.

"Probably a chest containing untold riches," said Po.

"OR THE EVOKER KING WAITING TO DESTROY US," Morgan suggested.

They all gave him a look.

"What?" he said. "I just want everyone to be prepared!"

"We're prepared," said Po. **"NOW BE A GOOD BOY AND DRINK YOUR POTION."**

Morgan tried to put his unease behind him. Even if they were swimming toward a trap, he had faith in his friends. And in the meantime, **he wanted to enjoy their time in the ocean.** It felt like being on another planet—one full of color and beauty and constant movement.

They passed school after school of fish. A squid swam across their path, unbothered by the sight of **strange four-limbed creatures.**

They were now farther than they'd ever traveled. Jodi found new blocks of coral to harvest. Ash

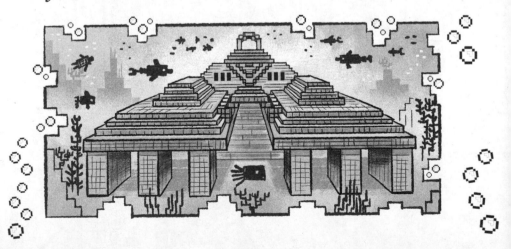

collected some kelp to dry out in a furnace later.

Then the ocean floor fell away. **The water got deeper.** And below them was a huge structure unlike any Morgan had seen before.

He'd read about structures like this, though. He knew an ocean monument when he saw it. **It was huge and built entirely of luminous**

green stone. There was something alien about it. It was beautiful, but also imposing.

He held up the map. The **X** was leading them right to the heart of that monument.

There was another, smaller structure nearby, built of the same green stone as the monument. It looked like a cube, but an incomplete one. He could see into its center, where **a glowing ball of energy swirled.**

It was a conduit, a rare underwater creation that had several impressive powers. Morgan knew that they would be able to breathe normally around it. **If they stayed close, they wouldn't need to drink any more potions or find any more bubble columns.**

He also knew that conduits, unlike monuments, did not generate naturally.

Someone had built it.

Before he could question why, he caught a glimpse of sudden movement out of the corner of his eye. He twirled around, hoping to see a dolphin.

It wasn't a dolphin.

Swimming toward Morgan was a fearsome

fish beast known as a guardian. **Its skin was greenish gray, and its bulky body was riddled with bright orange spikes.** Those spikes looked dangerous, as did its single red eye. With a flick of its fishtail, the monster was right on top of him.

Morgan swung his sword. **His attack was slowed by the water.** But he hit the guardian—and instantly wished he hadn't. As he slashed it, it slashed him back with one of its spikes.

The guardian retreated out of the reach of Morgan's sword. **Its eye flared with energy.** Morgan knew what that meant.

Laser!

Morgan dodged just in time. This thing meant business.

He swam toward it. **He raised his sword.** It would probably get him with its spikes again, but he didn't have any other way to repel it.

Or did he?

Before he could reach the guardian, Ash swam in front of him. She gestured madly for him to look down. He worried there was a second enemy below him. **But there was nothing scary down there.** Only their friends, huddled around the conduit.

The conduit! Ash was right!

Morgan remembered another of the conduit's powers. It would do more than allow them to breathe underwater. **It would also injure any hostile mob that came close to it.**

He just had to hope the guardian was mad enough to follow him.

Its eye glowed once more. **Ash shoved Morgan out of the way** of another laser beam.

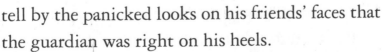

Ash kicked her legs and quicky swam toward the conduit. Morgan then followed closely behind her. He could tell by the panicked looks on his friends' faces that the guardian was right on his heels.

As they neared the conduit, **Morgan risked a backward glance.** The guardian was

nowhere to be seen. Had they lost it somehow?

Not looking where he was going, Morgan slammed right into Ash. She'd stopped swimming. He wondered why. . . .

And then he saw **the guardian right in front of her.** It had been fast enough to cut them off. Now it was blocking their path to the conduit.

The guardian's eye began glowing again. Morgan braced himself for the attack.

But then its whole body flashed red.

Once, twice, a third time.

The guardian was taking damage.

It had swum too close to the conduit, and it couldn't escape in time. After a few brief moments, the guardian was destroyed. All that remained of it was a floating, **twirling prismarine shard.** Morgan recognized it as the very material the ocean monument was built from.

He exchanged looks with the others. Everyone was okay, but they were shaken. **They hadn't expected to face a predator like that.**

Ash started placing blocks near the conduit. Her plan was clear. She wanted to create another shelter. That way, Morgan could heal and they could all rest before entering the monument.

Morgan was frustrated at the new delay. But he agreed with the plan.

There would probably be more guardians inside the monument. **And one boss battle per day was more than enough for him.**

Plus, it would be getting late in the real world by now. And he was starting to get pretty excited about their science project. **He wanted to check on his coral one more time before heading home for the day.**

Chapter 11

CORAL IS TRENDING. FRIENDSHIPS ARE ENDING!

Back in the real world, Harper nearly fell out of her seat when Po told them about his teammate's coral necklace.

She was eating lunch with her friends at their usual table. They were discussing their plan for exploring the ocean monument later that day. **Morgan expected there to be more of those monstrous fish inside.**

"It'll be a tough fight," he said. "But this time, we'll be ready. And then we can finally get back to land."

"Aw," said Jodi. "I never found a use for the coral I've collected."

"Why not bring it with you?" Harper asked.

"Morgan warned me what will happen if I use it out of the water," Jodi said. "It will all dry up and lose its color." She shrugged. "It belongs underwater."

Po slapped his own forehead. "That reminds me. You guys won't believe what Ricky was wearing the other day."

He was right. Harper really couldn't believe it.

"But that's terrible!" she said. "Coral isn't fashion; it's a living thing! The whole point of Doc's experiment is . . . **Oh no."** A terrible thought occurred to Harper. Hadn't it looked like one of her pieces of coral had gone missing?

"Po," she said. "Where did Ricky get the coral for his necklace?"

"I don't know," Po answered. "He said he bought it from a student. But, Harper . . . **It looked just like the coral from our experiments."**

That confirmed Harper's fear. "I think it was taken from my aquarium," she told them. "Someone is trying to ruin our experiment. I've got to warn Theo!"

Harper stood from her seat. She left her half-eaten sandwich on the table. She scanned the cafeteria and saw Theo at the far side of the room.

She started walking in his direction. But she'd only made it a few steps before **something caught her eye.**

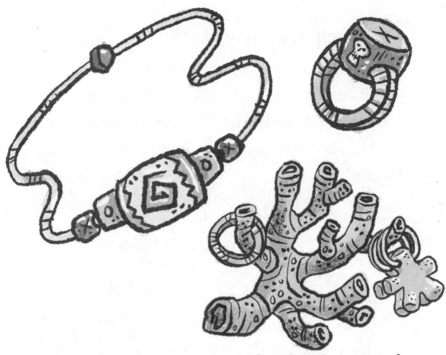

A classmate named Lisa had a coral necklace of her own.

Next to her, a kid named Jack sported a coral ring.

And Anna had a piece of coral adorning her yellow headband.

The corals were different shapes and colors. They weren't all from Harper's aquarium. But that wasn't much of a comfort.

"What are you all wearing?" Harper cried. "Are those coral earrings?"

"**Aren't they the best?**" said a boy named Giaco. "I'm asking my parents to order some for me. Check it out." He held up a smartphone. **It showed a website for coral jewelry.**

Harper's heart sank. "You can buy coral jewelry online?"

"Sure. Divers used to go looking for pearls," said Anna. "But pearls are so old-school. **Coral is going to be the next big trend.**"

"But that would be terrible," Harper explained. "Coral is a vital part of the planet's ecosystem! What you're wearing is basically the skeleton of a microscopic marine animal."

"**Wow! That is SO COOL!**" said Jack. And then he added in a confidential tone, "You're just making it sound better, you know."

"But this isn't right!" said Harper. "**Reefs provide a habitat—a home—for thousands of species of plants and animals.** Maybe *millions* of them! You're putting them all in danger."

"Well, yeah, but . . ." Lisa fiddled with her necklace. "*This* coral is already dead. So it's too late to do anything about it, right?"

"And if *they* have coral, shouldn't I be allowed to get some, too?" said Giaco.

Harper shook her head in dismay. She wasn't getting through to them.

She hurried over to her lab partner. "Theo,

you won't believe what's happened!" Harper said. **"Someone took coral from our aquarium.** And now a bunch of students are wearing coral like it's jewelry."

Theo's face broke into a wide smile. "That's great news," he said. **"My plan is working!"**

Harper narrowed her eyes. "Your plan?" she echoed. "What plan?"

"The coral jewelry was all my idea," Theo said. "I borrowed a piece from our aquarium and sold it to one of the basketball players. I knew he was a popular guy. **I hoped it would start a trend.** But I didn't think it would happen so fast!"

Harper was appalled. **"Why would you do that?"**

Theo's smile shrunk a little. "I . . . I could tell you were really worried about what's happening to coral reefs," he said. "But most people don't even know coral is in danger. **I thought if we showed people how beautiful it is, then they would want to save the reefs."**

"But now people are supporting businesses that are making the problem worse!" Harper said.

"What do you mean?" asked Theo.

"Divers are going into the ocean and taking chunks of coral. Whether they realize it or not, they're causing damage to reefs . . . and to the whole environment. And the more popular that jewelry gets, the more coral they'll collect and **the more damage they'll do!"**

Theo's smile dropped completely. "I didn't mean for that to happen," he said. **"I just wanted everyone to see that the coral was in trouble."** He ran his hands through his hair. "Can we fix this?"

Harper shook her head. "I don't think we can," she answered. **"Some problems are just too big to solve."**

Chapter 12

A MONUMENT TO WONDER!
TO SPLENDOR! TO . . .
ZOMBIE PIGMEN?

Jodi held up her sword the moment they entered the ocean monument. Morgan had told her to expect more guardians, and **she wanted to be ready.**

But she wasn't ready for what they found inside. Nothing could have prepared her for the sight.

Because inside the monument were **dozens of undead humanoid pigs** with gleaming swords.

"What are they?" Jodi whispered. She peeked around the corner for a better view.

"ZOMBIE PIGMEN," Morgan said gravely.

Po giggled. "Sorry," he said. "You just sounded

so *serious*. And those things are so weird."

Normally, Jodi and Po laughed at the same things. **But Jodi didn't find the pigmen funny.** They looked a little like pigs, but they walked on two legs. That would be creepy enough. But they were also rotting, undead things. Jodi could see gleaming white bones where their flesh had peeled away. Yuck.

She shuddered. "There's no way we can fight them all," she said.

"Fortunately, we don't have to," said Ash. "They aren't hostile."

"THE UNDEAD ANIMAL-PEOPLE HOLDING SWORDS AREN'T HOSTILE?" Jodi asked. "Are you sure?"

"Totally," said Morgan. "Watch." And he stepped around the corner, where the roomful of pigmen would be able to see him. They didn't even react.

"That's the good news," Ash said, and she joined Morgan among the pigmen. "BUT THERE'S A CATCH: ZOMBIE PIGMEN DON'T USUALLY SPAWN ANYWHERE BUT THE NETHER. So the

fact that they're here is another clue that someone is messing with the game. Messing with us."

"What's the Nether?" Jodi asked.

"A SCARY PLACE," Morgan answered. **"IT'S ANOTHER DIMENSION. ONE THAT IS BASICALLY ON FIRE."**

"Let's avoid that," said Po with mock seriousness.

They walked into the next room. The monument was huge, with high ceilings and tall columns. All of it was the same eerie green color. Except for the pigmen, it appeared empty.

"THIS IS ALL SO STRANGE," said Morgan. "This place should be full of water. It should contain guardians, like the one we fought yesterday."

"Look there," said Ash. "Prismarine."

Jodi saw what Ash was pointing to. It was a piece of green material.

"IT'S THE SAME MATERIAL THE GUARDIAN DROPPED AFTER IT WAS DESTROYED," Ash said. "Does that mean there *was* a guardian here? That someone already defeated it?"

"Oh man," Po said. **"SOMEONE BEAT US TO**

THE TREASURE, DIDN'T THEY?"

"Maybe. If that map was actually leading us toward treasure in the first place," Morgan said. "Let's keep looking around."

Jodi let her brother walk ahead of her. **She hung back to walk with Harper.** "Are you okay, Harper?" she asked. "You seem awfully quiet."

"I'm fine," Harper said. "Just lost in thought."

Jodi stopped walking, so Harper had to stop, too. **"YOU'RE DOING IT AGAIN,"** she said.

Harper looked confused. "Doing what?" she asked.

"You're worrying about a problem," Jodi said. "And instead of asking for help or even just talking to us about it, you're trying to put all the responsibility on your own shoulders. **BUT YOU DON'T HAVE TO FIX EVERYTHING, HARPER. YOU'RE NOT ALONE."**

Harper sighed. "Maybe you're right. I'm just thinking about that coral jewelry. I'm afraid Theo has started a trend that will cause a lot of damage."

"WELL, MAYBE WE CAN DO SOMETHING

ABOUT IT," Jodi said.

"Like what?" Harper said. "I've been trying to figure something out all day. I don't think it's possible to stop a trend."

"BUT TRENDS DIE ALL THE TIME," said Po. "They get replaced by new trends."

"And I don't think the coral jewelry will be popular for long," said Morgan. "It loses a lot of its color once you take it out of the water. Just like the coral Jodi took from the ocean here."

"AND IT'S FRAGILE," Ash said. "Half that jewelry is going to end up breaking. It's not durable, **LIKE METAL OR GEMSTONES."**

"That's kind of funny," Po said. "For once, fakes would actually be better than the real thing."

Jodi and Harper looked at each other.

"Are you thinking what I'm thinking?" Harper asked.

"THAT PO IS A SECRET GENIUS?" Jodi guessed.

"Uh, I am?" Po asked. He seemed to give it some thought before quietly deciding she was probably right. He was a genius.

"FAKE CORAL MIGHT BE JUST WHAT WE NEED!" Harper said. "We could create pieces that are more colorful and more durable than the real thing. Everyone could have coral jewelry, and **NO ACTUAL CORAL WOULD BE DESTROYED!"**

"And we'd get to make beautiful, colorful, unique pieces of art," Jodi said, bouncing on her feet. "All while raising awareness of the problems facing coral reefs. That's what Theo wanted to do in the first place."

Harper laughed. "I love it!" she said.

Jodi flushed with happiness. "See what happens when you talk it out?" she said.

But Morgan shushed her.

Jodi shot him a dirty look. "I was *just* talking about the importance of communication," she said crossly. "And you shush me?"

Then she saw that **Morgan's eyes had gone wide with panic.** He'd seen something in the next room that had frightened him.

"What is it?" Jodi whispered. "You look like you've seen a ghost."

"Not a ghost," Morgan said. **"A GHAST."**

And as if he'd summoned it, **a pale, menacing specter drifted in and hovered in the doorway.**

Chapter 13

PIGMEN, PIGMEN EVERYWHERE AND THEN THE GHAST DID BLINK

In all her years of playing Minecraft, **Harper had never visited the Nether.**

She knew it was a dark and scary place. It was full of dangerous mobs. And ghasts were perhaps the most dangerous of them all.

Zombie pigmen were out of place in the underwater monument. They were a puzzle.

But a ghast? Here? *That* was a trap. **Someone had lured them into a fight they might not win.**

The creature looked like a ghost, with a white body and dark slits for eyes. Nine large tentacles hung from its body as it drifted toward them.

"MAYBE IT'S NOT HOSTILE, EITHER?" said Jodi.

But Harper knew they wouldn't be so lucky.

She drew her sword just as the ghast shot a fireball at Jodi.

"GET BACK!" she cried, and she leapt in front of her friend. She swung her sword, and her timing was perfect. The rugged sword deflected the fireball, sending it soaring across the room.

For a moment, **Harper felt a thrill of triumph.** Then the fireball smashed into a group of zombie pigmen.

They flashed red with damage. They turned to look at her. And then they lifted their swords.

"They think you attacked them, Harper!" Ash warned.

"WE HAVE TO RUN!" said Morgan.

Morgan led the way, and Harper was right behind him. The pigmen followed in an undead stampede. **They grunted and growled.** The ghast moaned as it trailed behind them. Harper wished she could shut her ears to the terrifying noises.

She narrowly avoided a pigman's blade.

"Everyone, form a ring around Harper!" Ash cried. "The pigmen are only after her!"

A fireball crashed into the wall above their heads.

"Yeah, but the fire-breathing death squid is after all of us!" Po shouted.

"We have to keep moving," said Morgan.

As they hurried through the monument's vast halls, **their pursuers fell behind.** At first, Harper was relieved. *We can outrun them,* she thought. But she knew they couldn't run forever. Eventually, they'd come to a dead end.

They rounded one corner, then another. The sounds of the pigmen faded as the kids stepped into a large chamber. **There were wets sponges hanging from the ceiling.** But Harper's eyes were drawn to the doorway of darkest obsidian in the middle of the room. Within that doorway, the air rippled and glowed.

Harper gasped at the sight. **"A PORTAL TO THE NETHER!"** she said. "Is that where all those mobs came from?"

"It must be," Ash said. "Although **I WONDER IF THEY CAME OF THEIR OWN FREE WILL.** Or if someone brought them over . . ."

"Maybe we should break it," said Po. "Before anything else comes through."

"No!" Harper said. **"THIS IS JUST WHAT WE NEED."**

They all turned to look at her. "How is this a good thing?" asked Jodi.

"The pigmen are after *me.* If I travel to another dimension, they should stop being hostile. Then the rest of you will have a fighting chance against the ghast."

They all shouted their disagreement:

NO WAY.

IT'S TOO DANGEROUS.

YOU COULD RUN INTO MORE ENEMIES!

Harper silenced them with a wave of her hands. "It's the only way," she said. "I hit those pigman with the fireball. **I CAUSED THE PROBLEM. I HAVE TO FIX IT."**

Jodi stepped forward and took Harper's hand.

"Harper, haven't you learned anything?" she asked. "This is just like the coral problem. It's a problem that we all *share*. **SO WE SHOULD SHARE THE SOLUTION, TOO.**"

Harper hesitated. "Maybe . . . maybe you're right."

"She usually is," Morgan said. "Not that I like to admit it."

"IT'S ACTUALLY A GOOD PLAN," Ash said. "Except for the part where you're in the Nether alone."

"Should we all go through the portal?" suggested Po.

"I DON'T THINK SO," said Morgan. "If something went wrong, we'd be stuck. I don't like the idea of splitting up, but . . ."

"In this case, it makes sense," Po finished.

The hideous groans of the pigmen grew louder. The creatures would find them any moment now.

"I'll go with Harper into the Nether," Ash said quickly. "The rest of you can use the opportunity to stop that ghast."

"Do we have the firepower to do that?" asked Jodi. **"WE NEVER MADE MORE ARROWS. . . ."**

"I've actually got an idea about that," said Po. "It's an idea Harper gave me."

"See?" Jodi said to Harper. "What did I tell you?"

Harper nodded. **"TEAMWORK FOR THE WIN,"** she said. *I hope,* she thought.

Chapter 14

GREETINGS FROM THE NETHER! A BAD PLACE TO VISIT, A TERRIBLE PLACE TO LIVE!

Po watched as his friends Harper and Ash disappeared into the Nether.

"I hope they don't run into any trouble," he said.

"Right now, we have to focus on the trouble in *this* dimension," said Morgan. "I hope your plan works."

"Hey, guess what?" Po said. "Me too!"

"I CAN HEAR THE PIGMEN," Jodi warned. "They're just around the corner."

"We should lead them away from the portal," Morgan said. "Just in case."

Po nodded. **"LET'S DO THIS!"**

As soon as he rounded the corner, Po saw that the next room was full of zombie pigmen. **But they made no move to attack.** They seemed to have given up the chase as soon as Harper had disappeared.

"WHEW," he said. "Harper was right."

Then Morgan shoved him—just as a fireball came crashing to the ground.

"Up there!" Jodi cried. And Po saw the ghast

hovering in a far corner of the room.

"Okay," Po said. **"JUST LIKE WE PLANNED.
RUN!"**

Po took off running. He went in a circle around
the edges of the room. Morgan ran in the opposite
direction, while Jodi weaved all around the peaceful
pigmen.

The ghost appeared confused by all
the movement. It followed Jodi for a moment

but drifted the other way when it caught sight of Morgan. **It uttered a spine-chilling scream** that sounded to Po like the cry of an angry cat. Then it shot another fireball just as Po and Morgan passed each other.

They were moving too fast. **The fireball missed** them entirely.

It hit a zombie pigman instead. **The pigman burst into flames.**

And all the other pigmen turned angrily toward the ghast.

"Oh man," Po said. **"THAT THING IS TOAST."**

"Jodi!" Morgan cried. "Let's get out of here!"

As they fled the room, chaos erupted. The pigmen swarmed the ghast, which launched fireballs in rapid succession to defend itself.

The ghast was far stronger. But there were too many pigmen. There was no way the ghast could win.

Morgan, Po, and Jodi hurried back to the room with the portal. **Though the sounds of battle raged on, no mobs followed**

them. Morgan breathed a loud sigh of relief, and Jodi cheered. "Po, it worked!" she said.

"NOT THAT BATTLING ENDLESS MOBS DANGEROUS MONSTERS ISN'T FUN," Po said, taking a few breaths. "But I'm more than happy to let the pigmen do the hard part for us."

"THE OTHERS AREN'T BACK YET," Morgan said. "Should we go after them?"

Before Po or Jodi could respond, Harper and Ash poked their heads through the portal.

"Everything good in this dimension?" Ash asked.

"All clear," Po confirmed.

"Good," said Harper. **"BECAUSE YOU GUYS ARE GOING TO WANT TO SEE THIS."**

The Nether was every bit as frightening as Po had expected. The rocky terrain was uneven and surrounded with glowing, viciously hot lava. **Everything was the color of old blood.**

"This place gives me the creeps," Po said.

"That makes sense," Ash said. "It's not at all like home."

"Or is it?" Harper asked. She gestured toward the edge of a cliff. "Look down there."

Po and the others peered over the edge. **His jaw dropped** at what he saw below.

Minecraft was for building. Everybody knew that. **Given enough time and the right materials, a person could build pretty**

much anything here. A castle. A spaceport. Even a school.

"IS THAT . . . WOODSWORD MIDDLE SCHOOL?!" Morgan asked.

"Why would someone build a replica of our school?" said Jodi.

Po had a hunch. "Hey, Morgan? Do you still have that map?"

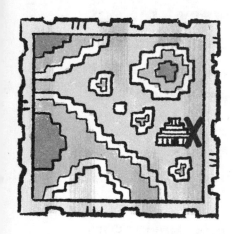

Morgan pulled out the map. Before, it had been a dull, faded yellow and orange. Now it was vibrant shades of red and orange. **The X was still there, too.**

"I've never seen that happen before," Morgan said. **"THIS MAP . . . IT'S BEEN LEADING US TO THE NETHER ALL ALONG."**

"It's been leading us *here*," added Ash. "Right to this spot. So that we would see that model of our school."

"It's a perfect re-creation," said Jodi. "Except for one thing—**OUR ACTUAL SCHOOL DOESN'T**

HAVE A BIG RED X ON ITS ROOF."

Po took another look. Jodi was right. The structure was built all in gray, except for several red blocks that gave the impression of an X. "What do you think that means?" he asked.

"IT MEANS THERE'S MORE TO THIS MYSTERY," said Harper. "And as much as I want to go down there and look around, WE'RE NOT EQUIPPED FOR THE NETHER YET."

"Yeah, and it's hot in here," said Jodi, wiping her brow and looking around nervously. "AND I BET THERE ARE LOTS MORE YUCKY-TYPE MOBS."

"We'll come back," Ash promised. "But in the meantime, I think this means we need to start looking for answers in the real world, too."

"I GUESS X REALLY DOES MARK THE SPOT," said Morgan.

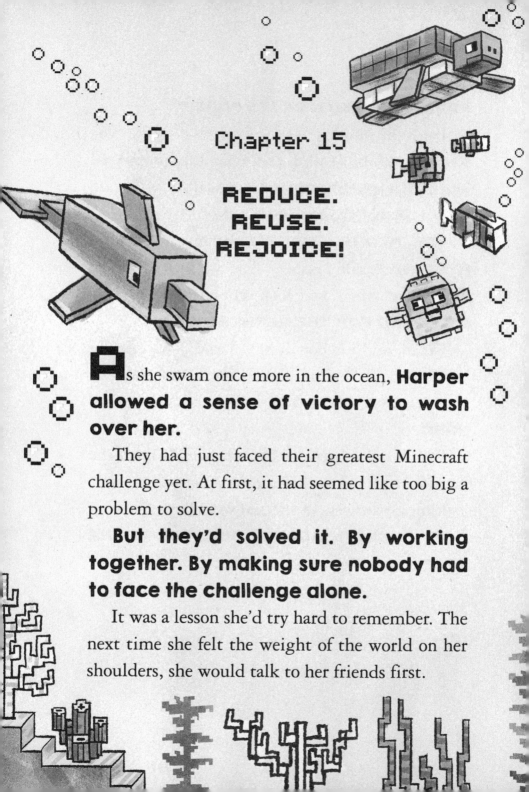

Chapter 15

REDUCE.
REUSE.
REJOICE!

As she swam once more in the ocean, **Harper allowed a sense of victory to wash over her.**

They had just faced their greatest Minecraft challenge yet. At first, it had seemed like too big a problem to solve.

But they'd solved it. By working together. By making sure nobody had to face the challenge alone.

It was a lesson she'd try hard to remember. The next time she felt the weight of the world on her shoulders, she would talk to her friends first.

A sea turtle was swimming nearby. Harper remembered those baby sea turtles they'd saved on the beach so many days ago. **Time moved quickly here.** Was this one of those babies, all grown up?

Protecting those hatchlings had been such a small action. But small actions had big consequences. **And enough small actions might add up to something truly great.** Maybe even saving-the-planet great.

Harper breathed a little easier. And this time, it had nothing to do with potions or a magical undersea conduit.

Ms. Minerva kicked open the door and entered the classroom. Doc was right behind her. Their arms were full of old lunch trays.

"Lunch is served!" called Doc. "Well, lunch trays, anyway . . ."

Harper hurried over to hold the door open for them. "Those are perfect," she said. "Are you sure we can use them, Ms. Minerva?"

"I'm absolutely thrilled about it," the teacher answered. She and Doc dropped the trays onto the table where Morgan, Ash, Jodi, and Po sat waiting. **"I told you, I don't want these things to end up in a landfill."**

"And we can't recycle them," said Doc. **"So giving them a new life is the next best thing."**

"A new life as jewelry," Harper said. She nodded. "We'd better get started."

"Could you use an extra set of hands?" asked Ms. Minerva.

"Always," said Jodi. "Pull up a seat!"

The seven of them worked all through the afternoon. At first, they followed Jodi's lead. **As the most experienced artist in the group, she had a lot of ideas for how to cut, reshape, and recolor the plastic trays into tiny, coral-inspired works of art.**

But as the afternoon went on, they all grew more confident. They began to experiment with new shapes and techniques. **Soon they had a small treasure trove of creations.** Those creations showed nearly as much variety and color as an actual coral reef.

"I already got the whole basketball team to agree to wear these tomorrow," Po said. "We know how good they are at starting a trend."

"Perfect," said Ash. "The more students who want to wear fake coral, the fewer who will buy the real thing."

"And that's good news for the environment," Harper said. She was the happiest she had been in days.

"Speaking of good news, I just got some," said Doc. She looked up from her smartphone. "I heard back from the coral research center. They've agreed to transport our lab-grown coral to a reef off the coast of Florida."

Jodi hopped from her seat. "You mean our coral is going to end up in the actual ocean? As part of an actual reef? Sweet!"

"Our little babies," Po said with an exaggerated sniff. "All grown up."

The friends laughed. **They exchanged high fives.** But then Harper saw a familiar face peeking through the window in the classroom door.

"Excuse me," she said. "I'll be right back."

She stepped out into the hallway. **Theo was there, looking unhappy.**

"What are you doing here so late?" she asked.

"Looking for you," Theo said. "I thought you'd be in the computer lab, like usual."

"Not today," Harper said. "We're making fake coral. I'm hoping it will convince kids to stop buying the real thing."

"So . . . you're trying to fix the mess I made," Theo said glumly.

"I'm not blaming you," Harper said. "I know you meant well, Theo."

"Maybe *you* know that," he said. "But what do your friends think? They probably think I did this on purpose. That I don't care about the environment."

"They're nice people," Harper said. "They don't judge anybody."

"Then can I join you all for Minecraft sometime?" Theo asked.

Harper hesitated. "We . . . don't really have an extra spot at the moment," she said at last.

"Yeah. That's what I thought you'd say." Theo pulled his backpack straps tight. "Well, you'd better hope I don't find a way onto your server," he said. "Because I could really spoil your fun."

Harper's mouth fell open as Theo walked away.

"Hey, are you okay?" asked Jodi. Harper turned to see her friends watching from the open classroom door.

"We didn't mean to eavesdrop," Morgan said. "But did he just say something about ruining Minecraft for us?"

"I don't think he meant it," said Harper. "He's just feeling a little hurt right now."

"Maybe," Morgan said. He rubbed his chin. "Or maybe we've found the Evoker King."

MINECRAFT is a game about placing blocks and going on adventures. Build, play, and explore across infinitely generated worlds of mountains, caverns, oceans, jungles, and deserts. Defeat hordes of zombies, bake the cake of your dreams, venture to new dimensions, or build a skyscraper. What you do in Minecraft is up to you.

Nick Eliopulos is a writer who lives in Brooklyn (as many writers do). He likes to spend half his free time reading and the other half gaming. He cowrote the Adventurers Guild series with his best friend and works as a narrative designer for a small video game studio. After all these years, Endermen still give him the creeps.

Luke Flowers is an author/illustrator living in Colorado Springs with his wife and three children. He is grateful to have had the opportunity to illustrate forty-five books since 2014, when he began his lifelong dream of illustrating children's books. Luke has also written and illustrated a best-selling book series called Moby Shinobi. When he's not illustrating in his creative cave, he enjoys performing puppetry, playing basketball, and going on adventures with his family.

JOURNEY INTO THE WORLD OF
MINECRAFT™

Learn about the latest Minecraft books when you
sign up for our newsletter at **ReadMinecraft.com**